Solo

Short Stories About Being Alone

James Olivieri

Table of Contents

Glaucus

It was a most unfortunate turn of events
which brought me to reside at the Emory Arms. My
education and experience in the field of finance
seemingly vanished with a most regrettable error in
judgment which caused me to be imprisoned for the
prior two years. At the time, I had just turned thirty-
five and had been returned to New York City
following my release from a prison upstate. My
clothing allowed me the façade of dignity that my
time in prison had made me long for. The designer
labels of my shirt and trousers stood in sharp
contrast to the fact that I had, only hours prior,
stepped off of a bus which I rode on a $40 ticket.
Perhaps worse yet, my crimes had cost me my job
and wife. I was back in the city I longed for, but I
was without a particular destination or a plan to
restore myself to the status to which I had grown
accustomed. Filled with pride and a desire to leave
behind that entire unpleasant phase of my life, I
sought no assistance in finding housing or work. I

was determined to find my own way, just as I had done when I came to New York as a student. What few worldly possessions I still possessed were kept in a cheap backpack, with the exceptions of the clothes I wore and the Tag Heuer watch on my left wrist. I had missed that watch. Upon arriving in prison it was taken from me by a oafish corrections officer who would have benefited greatly from a primer course in luxury timepieces.

"Is this watch worth more than $75?" he demanded.

"Worth more than $75? Sir, that watch is worth more than you." I had replied. It proved to be one of the many missteps I would take as I acclimated myself to institutional living. It was, perhaps, his unfamiliarity with the brand or perhaps a genuine dedication to his duty that caused the watch to be waiting for me upon conclusion of my sentence. This I took as a pleasant surprise as I reclaimed my property. But now, back in the city I loved and had missed more than anything else, I found myself with much to do and very few resources. Lodging was my most immediate concern. I knew that networking and job hunting could take weeks. I needed to find a place to live and had only the last $3,000 in my savings account to start a new life in a very expensive town. I don't think I fully appreciated how expensive New York City rent could be. While I knew I would be unable to return to my Upper West Side building, I had assumed, wrongly it seems, that I could find adequate housing in a chic downtown neighborhood. What I found was that the chic downtown neighborhoods were, in terms of rent, on par with the Upper West Side. I knew that I would be able to lodge for the night at any number of mid-town hotels. But, a one night stay would deliver quite a blow to my meager budget. Some clever searching from the computer of the public library brought me to the large brownstone on the lower east side. I entered the building and found myself standing in a historic, though decaying, foyer in a darkened building that smelled of must, body odor and disappointment. I knew the smell well from my first introduction to it on my first night in prison.

"Hello?" I called out. My call seemed to elicit a response as echoed footsteps were heard. A middle aged woman appeared moments later. She appeared tired and accustomed to work. Mildly impatient she was able to compose herself for my benefit before speaking.

"Can I help you?"

"Is this the Emory Arms?"

"It is. Can I help you?"

"I believe I spoke with you briefly on the phone. I'm Gerald."

"You want to see the room?" she asked with some doubt in her voice.

"That's correct." I confirmed. I noted that she seemed uneasy. Perhaps it was my attire or the affect to my voice. Prison was able to beat a significant amount of arrogance out of me, but I was not able to hide my education or the mannerisms I had crafted over the years. She gestured for me to follow as she began up the massive wooden staircase. We passed worn hallways and ratty carpeting as we made our way to the fourth floor of the building.

"Every floor has two bathrooms. One on the north end of the hallway and the other on the south. For the courtesy of other residents, showers lasting more than ten minutes are prohibited. Your rent includes the room and all utilities. You can get cable, but you pay that." she spoke without looking to me as she opened the door to the corner room on the fourth floor. "Every room is guaranteed to have at least one window, a sink and a bed. This room has two windows, so it costs $10 per week more." she continued as she gestured for me to enter. The floor was hardwood and in severe need of refinishing. The twin sized bed was an old metal frame with a rolled up mattress bundled in the center. A wooden chair sat near the old fashioned sink and the only electric light in the room was provided by an exposed light bulb dangling from the center of the ceiling. The one redeeming quality of the room was the fact that there were two windows, one on each exterior wall that allowed a more than adequate amount of natural light into the dreary room.

"And how much is it?" I asked as I looked around.

"It's $185 per week, including the charge for the extra window." She responded. I was less than impress with the accommodations, especially for the price. It is worth noting that boarding houses are becoming increasingly scarce, especially in New York these days. Thus, it seemed my only options were to live here or to attempt to pay the outrageous rent of a space not much better, but with the benefit of a private toilet.

"I'll take it." I found myself saying.

"I need a one week deposit at least." the woman said as she pulled the key from her pocket, a cardboard tag with the room number written on it was attached. Reaching into my pocket I pulled out my wallet. I had taken $1,000 from the bank in anticipation of getting myself established. I gave her $740 of that to pre-pay the entire month.

"Here you are." I said as I took the key from her hand.

"And I thank you for agreeing to show me the place on such short notice." She didn't acknowledge my thanks. She only counted the money and tucked it into her pants pocket. She withdrew a receipt pad from a back pocket and scrawled out a receipt, which she signed, before tearing off the top copy and handing it to me.

"I'll be back on the first of the month. It's better if you come and find me before I start looking for you."

"I will do just that then." I said. She seemed to be reassured, or at least satisfied for the moment, she departed the room and resumed her cleaning duties of the common areas. No background or credit check was done. As I looked at the receipt, I found she had butchered the spelling of my last name. Sighing I closed the door and tossed my backpack on the metal frame. Grabbing the back of the wooden chair, I spun it to face the window exposed to the street and I sat, looking out at the people as they milled about.

"Tonight I rest. Tomorrow, I find work." I said aloud. With my mission for the day accomplished, I felt some sense of relief within my stomach. I knew that, at the very least, I had a place to sleep at night. If tomorrow went as well as today did, I could count on finding employment and working to rebuild the life I had left on the other side of that prison sentence.

The next few days were wrought with disappointment. I found that my professional network had cast me out and former friends no longer seemed willing to acknowledge my very being. This proved a time of house cleaning whereby I learned who among them I could still count among my friends. Through a former business associate, I was able to secure a position well below the level to which I had risen before the unpleasantness that landed me in prison. I was essentially a shipping clerk. Though this position didn't really pay the level I was used to, it was enough to make rent and buy food while maintaining health insurance with very few discretionary dollars to spare. For now, I would have to settle for my position on the lower end of Maslow's hierarchy until I could build myself up once again. Every night, I would conclude my work and walk home to keep expenses low. I enjoyed this walk through a part of town I had not previously known. I enjoyed the stimulation of lights and sounds that would end when I arrived at my simple peasant lodgings in the midst of a wealthy Manhattan. I would sit in the wooden chair and examine my room for inspiration. I had studied every bit of peeled paint and every water stain. I found it odd that, in a building with so many inhabitants in a city of millions, I could be so utterly alone and isolated. I had known this feeling while imprisoned as well. So now, as I had then, I retreated to a book of Greek mythology that had carried me through the toughest of nights in the state prison. I had fallen in love with the Hellenic gods when I was in high school. The tales of their heroism and the wrath that resulted from their jealousy thrilled me more than the typical social activities of a young man of my age. One of the greatest thrills of my life came when I had the opportunity to tour the ruins of the ancient temples while still in college. I imagined a time when I might have stood at the Acropolis prepared to bring my sacrifice before Athena for the protection and benefit of my family. It was a silly notion, I suppose. I had never been religious. My father was an atheist while my mother was a spiritualist. I did not set foot inside a church until my own wedding. I had no reason to believe that I would have been a religious man in the time when Zeus was said to have reigned. I read my book with ankles propped up near an open window. As thoughts of ancient heroes and temple ceremonies filled my mind, I found my eyes closing to better enable the fantasy to run free. I cannot describe that initial feeling. It was as if a thought occurred to me that had been so obvious I was embarrassed for not having thought of it sooner. My eyes opened and looked around the pitiful room. My feet lowered to the floor as I set the book on the thin mattress.

"Athena, Protectress of Athens. I call to you in humble supplication." I said aloud in a melodic tone. "They say you have fallen and no longer rule from your seat on Olympus. If you can hear my words, please give me a sign." Then I didn't speak and found myself holding my breath. There was silence in the room. Of course there was silence. What else would there be? I shook my head at my own silliness in attempting to invoke a mythological being. I reached up and rubbed the back of my head as I rose from my chair and went into the hallway. I began down the darkened corridor to the nearest bathroom. Once inside I closed the door as I readied myself to go to bed. It was there at the bathroom mirror, having just brushed my teeth, that I saw a movement in the bathroom window. As I walked closer, I was able to ascertain that a bird was perched just outside the glass. As I moved closer, I realized how truly peculiar a situation this was. I had expected to see a pigeon or maybe even a seagull that had wandered to lower Manhattan. But perched there, looking in at me was a white owl. Its beauty was striking. But it was the images of Athena with an owl perched on her shoulder that caused me to gasp and quickly open the window. I'm not sure what I expected the owl to do. But as I opened the window, the owl flew away. I quickly closed the window and returned to my room, closing the door behind me. I clasped my hands together as I sat on the bed. "Athena, Goddess of War and Wisdom, I have seen your sign. Thank you." I didn't know what else to say. I stood to turn off the naked light bulb before easing back onto the bed and reclining. I didn't know what to think of the owl situation. Perhaps it was a coincidence, but perhaps there was something more to this.

The following day I left work under grey skies with a light misty rain filling the air. I left work with unusual fervor as I proceeded along the Bowery toward my depressing little room. As I hurried through the chilly mist I found myself stopping just two blocks away as I stared at the white owl perched on a storefront's awning on a side street. I pulled the cheap blue windbreaker, a parting gift from the state prison, around my body tighter as I trotted across the street to get a better look at the owl. As I approached the storefront, the owl flew off further down the side street. I found myself jogging to keep up with it. The owl came to rest upon a metal railing beside a blue door. There was an "open" sign in the door's glass panel but no other signage to indicate the business therein. I slowly wrapped my hand around the brass handle and turned it. Finding no resistance from a lock, I looked back at the owl for reassurance before pulling the door open and slipping inside. The store was simple yet clean and well organized. The smell of unburned incense and spices filled my nostrils as I moved to the counter. There, a woman around my age sat beside a cash register as she read a book. Seeing me enter she smiled.

"Hello, can I help you find anything?"

"I'm...not sure what it is I'm looking for." I said. It seemed a more reasonable response than telling her that a white owl had guided me into the store.

"Well we have a little bit of everything. Have you just begun studying new age philosophy?"

"I haven't really studied anything of the sort, to tell you the truth. For quite a while I have studied the Greek pantheon. I started reading it again last night. I was walking home today and…happened upon your store here."

"Well I'm glad you did. I think you'll find quite an interesting selection over here." she hopped down from her stool behind the counter and walked over to an opposite wall. I felt compelled to follow her as she directed me to a section of bookshelves. There, hanging above the crammed shelves was a picture of Athena's statue beside the words "Greek Religion." I found my eyes almost immediately drawn to a book on the modern worship of the Greek Gods. This, I reasoned, could be what the owl had intended to show me. I turned the book over several times in my hands before flipping idly through the pages. The shopkeeper merely stood by looking on with a smile.

"That's a good one. I think if you are taking your study into practice that is the best way to go."

"I'm not sure I want to practice anything. I've gone my entire life without any real religion."

"Well, something brought you here. Isn't there something you are lacking in your life? Something that maybe a higher spirit can help you achieve?"

"You mean to say that Zeus will help me get a better job? Maybe help me get a better place?"

"I don't know. Maybe. Or maybe you'll find that those things aren't what you need after all."

I flipped the book around in my hands a few moments longer. My eyes caught sight of the price tag. At $25, this book would nearly deplete any discretionary cash I had for the remainder of the month. I could dip into savings, but I was trying to avoid that except in the likely even of an emergency. Reaching into my pocket I fished out $30 and handed it to the woman.

"Well then, I imagine I'd be a fool not to buy it." She smiled and took my money to the register, meeting me halfway to return my $3 in change. I thanked her for her help and stepped back outside. There, I could see the owl still perched on the railing. "Is this it?" I asked. The owl simply flew upward out of my sight. I took that to mean that I had acquired the appropriate book.

I continued my travels home and, as on other nights, I settled into the unsteady wooden chair and propped my feet up on the window after pushing the window to an open position. I began to read the pages carefully. I was both excited and somewhat afraid of the new knowledge I was gaining. I was also aware that it was unlikely the owl was guiding me to a relaxing read. I felt that this was likely a sign that I was meant to practice the rituals in this book.

It took me some weeks to gather the appropriate supplies that were outlined in my new text. For the time being, I could only offer verbal praise to the unseen deities that seemed to take a keen interest in me. In bits and pieces I finally came to acquire the necessary goods. I now had a miniature statue of Athena and a small brass bowl for libations. I purchased the best wine I could afford, which was rather cheap, and I had found a small end table on the curb that would serve as my altar. At work that morning, I had just applied for a promotion to the position of shipping supervisor. While it was hardly a fast-track to riches, it would alleviate my material concerns without my having to dip into savings, or sell my watch. But that was a matter I could worry about another time. Having seldom entered a church and only recently begun to pray, I stood in my room wearing a tank-top shirt and cheap work trousers holding a bottle of wine in my hands.

"Hear me, Athena. Your servant calls out to you." I said aloud as I closed my eyes. "I bring you this offering to satisfy your thirst and pray that you bless me with your countenance. Bring me wisdom and strength. Help me to overcome my foes and restore me to my proper place." I spoke in a monotone, closing my eyes for a moment before I approached the altar. I poured wine into the brass bowl before speaking again."I consecrate this wine to you, Athena and pray that you accept my offering." as I spoke, I felt a rush of wind sweep through the street view window. I heard the distinct sound of flapping wings and turned to see the white owl perched on my sill. I knew this to be a sign that my offering was acceptable. I set the bottle of wine down and picked up the bowl. My book of worship indicated that I could not dispose of the liquid in an unclean manner such as pouring it down the sink. Ideally, one would pour it into the ground where it might be returned to the earth. But in the heart of Manhattan, I would have to carry this bowl for quite a ways before I found a suitable patch of grass. Instead, I set the bowl on the window sill beside the owl and sat in my chair. The owl lowered its beak to the wine, seeming to be examining it. Then it flapped its wings and flew away once again. I turned out my light and allowed the glow of the city to guide me to my bed. As I lay on my back I felt that, for the first time since my conviction, the tides were turning in my favor.

The following morning when I reported to work, I was summoned to my manager's office. I was informed that I had received the promotion for which I had applied and I would be taking on the responsibilities of shipping supervisor at the end of the week. The raise was minimal but the responsibilities were greater. The new job seemed to promise more mental stimulation, if nothing else. The rest of the day went by with relative ease and I found myself, around 3 p.m. that day, beginning to think of nothing more than going home and offering another libation to Athena. That day, as I proceeded home along the route I had grown fond of over the past few weeks, I began to contemplate the others things I would enjoy. I resolved to ask next for a reunification with my wife, who had divorced me in prison to spare her dignity in the eyes of family and friends. I was so happy with this sudden turn of events that I nearly ran up the aged stairs to my room. After a usual routine of a shower, I set up my altar for another devotion. The brass bowl still contained liquid, having not evaporated as readily as I had assumed. I looked around for a place to deposit the liquid and remembered a potted tree in the foyer of the building. I carefully carried the libation bowl to the ground floor before pouring the liquid into the soil of the plant. I returned to my room and placed the bowl on the altar. Resuming my bottle of wine I chanted as I had done once before.

"Hear me, Athena. Your servant calls out to you. I bring you this offering to satisfy your thirst and pray that you bless me with your countenance. Thank you for the blessings which you have bestowed upon me. If it is within your grace, I pray that you reconcile me with my wife." I smiled as I made my pleading. I poured wine into the brass bowl as I had done the prior night and then moved the bowl to the window sill. Sitting in my chair, I smiled as the white owl's wings fluttered and he came to perch himself beside the bowl. I felt warmth within me knowing that my sacrifice had again been accepted. And so I began a nightly ritual of giving praise to Athena. Each night, I received a visit from the owl to accept my offering.

After about a week, I discovered a white envelope in my mail slot in the foyer. I was delighted to see that it had been written by Connie, my ex-wife.

Dear Gerald;

It has been a difficult year for me. My therapist recommended that I write you this letter to better express these emotions. Your conviction ruined us as a family and has left me financially and emotionally bankrupt. I have been depressed and at times felt completely hopeless. While I cannot forget the hurt you have caused me, I wanted to let you know that I forgive you.

Sincerely,

Connie

I smiled as I read the letter. Though it was hardly the full reunion I had hoped for, it was a step toward full reconciliation. That night, as on others, I offered my same libation to the Goddess Athena. My confidence grew as my prayers were answered. I had fallen to the lowest point of my life but I was now working on a triumphant rise. Reunion with my wife would mean a return to my uptown apartment and restoration of most of the wealth I had accumulated in the days leading up to my trial. Continued promotions at work would mean additional responsibilities and more money. Though I doubted I could rise to the executive level at this company, it could well provide enough resume fodder to enable me to re-launch my career. I had been molded into my successful self in the classrooms of New York University. I was tempered by the fires of Wall Street. And now from the ashes, I would rise from room 410 of the Emory Arms Rooming House on the Lower East Side of Manhattan.

My correspondence with Connie was slow but regular. Three months after that initial card of forgiveness, I found myself seated at dinner with my ex-wife in the designer clothes I wore out of prison and now saved for occasions such as this. It had been nearly six months in total since I was released from prison and aside from this dinner and my visit to the bookstore under the guidance of the white owl; I was only ever to be found at the Emory Arms, my job or in transit in between those two points. It was perhaps for this reason that I felt especially uncomfortable being out of the routine I had carved out for myself. I was also filled with adrenaline as I had recently applied for the position of shipping manager and expected to learn of the decision the following day. I smiled as I looked to Connie.

"So tell me about your job." she asked.

"I'm a shipping supervisor. I can't say that it is Wall Street, but it keeps my mind busy and pays the rent."

"How is living in the East Village? I remember when I was a kid my mother used to talk about it being a bad neighborhood."

"It's up and coming." I reassured with a smile.

"I'm thinking of selling the apartment. The maintenance has become too much on my salary. I'm only scraping by now because my parents are helping me out."

"It's a buyer's market; you could probably turn a profit if you hold onto it for a bit longer."

"I don't know that I have that much longer. I didn't realize how little I was making as a teacher until you went...away." she avoided mentioning prison. I couldn't help but wonder whether her intent was to spare my dignity or her own.

"Well for the time being, why not hold onto it? I mean, who knows, maybe one day I'll be back." I said slyly.

"Look, Gerald. I'm really glad I don't hate you anymore. And I'm really glad you don't hate me. But I can't forget what you put me through. I like you again, but I don't love you. And to tell you the truth, I can't imagine ever falling in love with you again. The repercussions of your actions are still being felt today. I am still being punished for what you did." she said. Her tone was as gentle as it could be considering the blow she had to deliver. The words stung but I was able to hold it together. We parted ways soon afterward and I began a very long walk from the mid-town restaurant to the Emory Arms. I realized as I walked that I had no right to complain. I did ask for reunion and we had reunited over dinner. Perhaps my request wasn't specific enough. More likely, it was as the woman in the bookstore had said, what I wanted wasn't really what I needed. My pride was hurt, but I was determined to carry on.

"I know I have no right to complain. You have showered me with gifts and I offer you only a modest wine. I am grateful for your blessings, Athena. I will work harder to show you my devotion." I said aloud as I walked down the street. Once I returned to the security of my room, I offered my nightly libation with the last drops of wine in the bottle. I would have to buy more tomorrow. I felt a brief knot in my stomach as I remembered I may well be buying that new wine on the promise of a raise and a promotion. I tried to put that out of my mind for the evening as I settled into much needed sleep.

I found myself thinking about the promotion for the majority of the morning. When my call to the manager's office came, my heart seemed to skip a beat. I walked into the office and sat down.

"Morning, Gerry. How are things going out there?"

"They're going well. And yourself, sir?"

"Going all right, going all right." the older man shuffled some papers on his desk as he spoke.

"I like you, Gerry. You've got more education than the people who run the company and you do great work here. Since I'm retiring I was kind of hoping to put you into my place. But the powers that be don't like your criminal record. They don't like it at all. I get that people make mistakes, I really do. But the big wigs don't like the idea of promoting an ex-con who's been here less than a year. I'm sorry, Gerry, my hands are tied. But after that year passes, look out, brother. I think they're gonna put you somewhere nice." I nodded as I folded my hands in my lap. I was disappointed to be sure. The disappointment would likely not have hurt as badly had I not received a similar rejection from Connie the night before. A fleeting thought caused me to doubt the whole divine intervention. But I shook my head; the white owl was guiding me on behalf of Athena. I couldn't possibly get everything I wanted whenever I wanted it. Were that the case, all of ancient Greece would have known untold fortunes. I thanked my manager for his consideration before I returned to work. When I left for the day, I found myself in need of another bottle of wine. I decided to buy the more expensive bottle even though I wasn't being promoted. I went home to the room I was beginning to appreciate more and more and offered my libation. I sat backwards in the wooden chair, resting my chin on the backrest as I watched the white owl approach the window.

"What's next for me, Athena? All I want is to be restored to my former station in life. I thought

I was on my way. Must I wait longer? Please tell me where I am meant to go." I asked of the white owl. After inspecting my wine as it always did, it flew away. But unlike the other days, it did not fly upward and out of my sight. Instead, the owl flew across the street to perch on a metal railing. I took the hint as I grabbed my blue windbreaker and pulled it on. I rushed down the stairs and began to follow the owl as it again moved from spot to spot, careful not to lose me as I followed. I found myself moving at a jog to keep pace with the owl as it made its way west across the city.

So enthralled was I in the pursuit, that when I finally came to stop, I leaned forward with hands resting on my knees as I panted. I looked around and only then began to realize just how far the owl had taken me. From my humble room on the Lower East Side, I now stood before the Washington Square Arch. I returned my gaze to the owl which had come to rest on a black metal railing near a well-tended dog park in Washington Square Park. As I approached the dog park, the owl took flight again. I continued to follow, though at a decidedly more leisurely pace as it led me to the Northwest corner of the park. There the messenger of Athena would perch on the branches of what was known as the hangman's elm. I came to know this historic tree during my studies at New York University. It had once been rumored that the city's hangings from years ago took place from the boughs of this very elm. Though the legends were later refuted by historians, the tree retained its name. I tucked my hands in my pockets as I looked up to the white owl and I smiled. That was when I fully came to understand the plan laid out before me by the Gods and Goddesses of the Hellenes. I was filled with elation as I came to gaze upon the tapestry of destiny woven to me by the nimble hands of the moirai. As my revelation took hold within my mind, I watched as the owl flew away out of my view. At first I considered a stroll in Washington Square Park, the place where I had first met Connie while we were both students, but I decided instead to make the long trek back to my room at the Emory Arms.

And so here I stand at the threshold of my destiny. I realized that Athena had delivered into my hands my means of restoration. At present, I am a convicted felon without name or reputation within the community. My errors have cost me material wealth and the respect of my peers. On my present path, the obstructions of the past forty-eight hours would prove to be the rule rather than the exception. I will continue to be rejected by my former wife. I will continue to be denied promotions or economic opportunity based solely on my term in prison. To walk straight ahead would mean a path of humility as I slowly faded into obscurity like the prior inhabitants of my room at the Emory Arms. But I stand now at a cross-road. At this intersection, I find myself no longer desiring to walk straight ahead along a road of broken dreams and unfulfilled desire. Simply turning to the side will be my redemption. I am amazed at how steady my hands have been as they slipped the rope around my neck.

I cannot believe that my legs did not quiver as I climbed atop the wooden chair. In life I am destined to slowly rot in this forgotten room located within a dilapidated building in the bowels of New York City. In death, Connie's economic woes would be relieved as she is the beneficiary of my life insurance policies. Policies, I might add, that had a two-year suicide exclusion which had long since passed. In the graveyard my crimes will be forgotten and my felony conviction will never be mentioned. I will lie beside men and women of my former station, joining them once again as an equal. I place a coin under my tongue to pay my fee to Kharon as I look up to observe the white owl sitting on my window sill.

"Lady Athena, I thank you for your beneficence and pray that you will see me delivered safely to Elysium." I say aloud as I now take my final step from the surface of the wooden chair.

Purgatory

The ticking of the wall clock's second hand was the only sound that broke an otherwise eerie silence. Three friends sat in a living room as they had many times before. The only difference now was that they sat there with only eternity before them. Frederick sighed as he began to tap his fingers on the arms of his chair in rhythm with the clock's ticking. He glanced at the clock as he had done many times during the course of his life, though now the clock had no hour hand. The three friends could only watch as seconds and minutes ticked by, and wait for an unknown moment at the end of an indefinite period.

"Do you think we're supposed to be doing?" Simon asked. He wore a black pinstripe suit and his left hand delicately held a glass of burgundy. He idly swirled the liquid, watching it as he spoke.

"If Catholic theology holds true, then we should be purging our souls of sin. But I should think we might get some guidance on doing that," Frederick said.

"Unless we're in Hell," Harris added.

"It can't be Hell. We have everything we could ever want. We have comfortable accommodations, wine, food and company. We're bored but we aren't really suffering," Frederick countered.

"Not yet, but if we have to sit here waiting for eternity, that sounds pretty damning to me. Harris said. "We've already run out of things to talk about. We've read all of the books. We've tasted every wine and eaten every cheese. Maybe thinking you've made the cut is part of the punishment. Maybe the disappointment of realizing that this is as good as it gets is what Hell is." He was almost disturbingly void of emotion as he spoke.

Frederick rose from his chair and walked to the large window that had once looked out upon a quiet middle class street. He grabbed the curtains in both hands and pulled them open. Outside the house everything was pitch black. One could see neither sky nor ground. Breaking through the black abyss was the lurid glow of fire emanating from a pit carved out of the nothing. Flaming arms and heads could be seen struggling to escape from the pit, only to fall back moments later.

"You know, Harris, I think that things could somehow be worse. If nothing else, let's be grateful that we are here and not there, Frederick said dryly.

"Grateful to whom?" Harris demanded.

"To God," Frederick said.

"But two of us were atheists in life," said Simon. "So why should we have been spared in the first place if there is a God? I have two theories. The first is that this place is a creation of our own mind. Let's say that there is no God. So the three of us departed life and somehow we created this space. We staked a claim in the void and created it. That would mean that neither the pit of fire to the house's north nor the white glow to the south is anything more than an image, a backdrop for our creation.

The second theory would be along the lines of what Frederick proposed before -- Namely that there is a God and that this God was merciful to us despite our non-belief during our lifetimes. I will expand on that notion and say that perhaps, if there is a God, he is not necessarily the God we learned about growing up. This may be a God of physics, bound by order and showing no particular mercy or wrath. We may be here simply because this is where the order dictates we land. We may progress toward the pleasant light. We might regress into the pit of fire. Perhaps we are bound to spend our eternity right here between the two."

"There's another theory we haven't really considered," Harris began. "What if we aren't even here? What if the accident left one or all of us comatose and this place is all a delusion."

"Then that, I would say, is an argument for us trying to move toward the light." Frederick said.

For a few brief moments, the monotony of the house was broken. The three enjoyed their discourse. Though, in the backs of their minds, they knew it would come to an end before too long. Whether the conversation lasted for an hour or for ten, it didn't seem to matter. With no real sense of time and with nothing to look forward to, the minutes all blurred together. These conversations had become a welcome respite from the ceaseless boredom that had become the reality for the three men. They had been friends since high school in a life long gone. They were together when they ended their respective lives in a car that was unable to traverse the icy roads safely on their last night. Since then, they found themselves in an immortal version of Frederick's mortal home. Frederick, Simon and Harris, who had once been a theologian, an economist and a physics teacher, respectively, during the course of their short lives, had each other's company and a house with unending supplies with which to occupy themselves for an indefinite period of time.

"I'm going to bed," Frederick said as they reached the end of their conversation. Behind him,

Harris and Simon continued to idly converse as he made his way up the stairs of the modest home as he had done many times at the conclusion of lively discussions with his friends.

He entered the master bedroom as he had done every night since purchasing the house. With the arrival of his two housemates, he had lost the rest of the space. Then again, he didn't seem to need needed guest rooms or a place to store his bicycle anymore. He removed the button-down shirt slowly and tossed it into a hamper as he sat on the edge of his bed. He looked up at the certificates on the wall above his desk. Those diplomas indicated that he was both a master in his field and a doctor of his chosen discipline of theology. Not that it mattered here and now. His friends had likewise achieved academic and career success, Harris in the sciences and Simon in economics. But they no longer had a place to teach or students to engage. The three of them had only one another to pontificate to and more time than things to say.

Frederick removed his shoes and climbed under the sheets. He closed his eyes for what seemed to be a moment, only to open them again soon after. He didn't know if only seconds had passed or if he had been asleep for days.

He climbed out of his bed and got dressed and walked downstairs, where he found his two friends seated just where he had left them.

"How long was I asleep?" Frederick asked.

"Who the hell knows?" Simon responded. "It felt like you only just left. I went to refill my wine and you came back down only seconds after I sat back down. Or maybe a thousand years passed in the interim."

Frederick nodded in reply and walked into the kitchen. Opening the large stainless steel refrigerator door, he looked over the well-stocked shelves that never seemed to empty. His fingertips danced over the various containers before settling on one filled with uncooked shrimp.

"Does anyone want some shrimp?" Frederick called out.

"Not hungry!" Simon replied. Frederick smirked as he reserved a remark about Simon's portly stature.

"No, thank you," Harris said. Frederick idly listened to Simon and Harris as they talked about the political situation of a country that no longer mattered to any of the three men. But Frederick turned his attention from fiscal policies to the raw crustaceans before him as he contemplated which method of preparation would yield the tastiest treat. Then Frederick came to the realization that he was not hungry either. As he thought back, he understood that he hadn't actually been hungry for quite some time. But it seemed so normal to eat after going to sleep; he hadn't given it much thought before. He walked into the living room and rubbed the back of his neck.

"When was the last time you guys were actually hungry or thirsty?" Frederick asked.

"I don't remember, Harris replied. He sounded intrigued by the question.

"I'm often thirsty," Simon said.

"Are you thirsty, or are you drinking that wine because that's what you always used to do when you came over to my house before?" Frederick asked.

"I don't know. I guess I never really gave it much thought," Simon said. He looked down into his wine glass. He took a sip and swished the liquid around in his mouth for a moment before swallowing. "You know, it doesn't actually taste like anything. " The other two men trusted Simon's judgment in the matter. In life, Simon wouldn't wear a tie unless its label could clearly betray its exorbitant price. He drank wine daily to develop a palate that would eventually become the envy of his wine club. He was regarded as brilliant in his lifetime for his perceptive mind which quickly made sense of everything which was observable to the senses.

Armed with this knowledge, Frederick walked into the kitchen and threw open the refrigerator door. He pulled out two containers and set them on the granite countertop, pulling off the lids, and tossing them aside. Harris and Simon entered the kitchen to watch. Frederick closed his eyes and placed a raw shrimp in his mouth, followed by a steamed carrot. He opened his eyes and slid the container closer to his friends as he chewed.

"Go ahead, try it. Neither of them tastes like anything." Frederick said. The other two men seemed unsure as they ate the contents of the containers.

"Tasteless. I can't even distinguish the textures," Simon said.

"Frederick, are you actually tired when you go to bed, or do you just go to bed because that's what you've always done?" Simon asked.

"Do you two ever feel tired?" Frederick replied. Harris and Simon looked to one another and then back to Frederick. Both shook their heads.

"All right," Frederick said. "Here's a theory. Maybe we are here to realize we don't need the things we valued while we were alive."

"What would the point of that be?" Harris asked. Harris was a skeptic. He scrutinized each passing moment of their afterlife as if trying to uncover a hoax. If Simon was the expert of the material, then Harris was the resident scholar of the immaterial. Though he believed in no God, he believed in the order of a mathematical world.

"You know how people always talk about what they want in heaven? How they hope there is beer or fishing? They hope you can fix up old cars or live in a mansion?" Frederick asked.

"But you don't actually need those things when you're dead. Mansions are places where people live, not where the dead spend their eternity." Simon replied. He set his wine glass down on the counter beside the tasteless shrimp.

"Exactly. Maybe we're here to cast off those worldly notions before we can move on?" Frederick said. For the first time, in an indefinable period, Frederick felt a mental excitement that began in his first year of college and ended following the final lecture he delivered before his death. Though he lacked the scientific order of Harris, he was capable of looking beyond the physically observable, unlike Simon.

"I think it more likely that we have reached a certain point of lucidity and think this speaks to my coma theory," Harris added.

"Either way, I think we need to keep going with this line of thinking," Simon said.

There was silence as the three men stood in the kitchen. Then Frederick pulled his wallet from his pants pocket and dumped the contents onto the counter. His hand sifted through everything briefly. His life was summarized in a series of identification and membership cards. He pushed them into the kitchen sink and looked to the other two. Simon was the first to react. He removed his own wallet from his coat pocket and dumped the contents directly into the sink. He removed the designer watch and the fraternity ring and dropped them in as well.

"I think you guys might be taking this a bit literally. I don't think we need to do this," Harris said.

"I think this is exactly what we need to do," Frederick replied.

"What if it doesn't work? We're going to destroy everything in our pockets for nothing."

"Who cares? What do you need a driver's license for now? When was the last time you paid dues to an association? If your theory is correct, then this is all in our heads anyway. What does it matter if we burn these things? They will only be waiting for us when we wake up," Simon said.

Harris sighed as he nodded slowly. It made logical sense. He took out his own wallet and threw it into the sink. Simon reached into his pocket to retrieve his designer lighter. With a flick of his thumb, the soft flame began to burn. He simply dropped it into the sink with the other belongings. Frederick meanwhile made his way upstairs and took the certificates down from his bedroom wall. He rushed to the kitchen and dropped them into sink. The fire quickly engulfed them and provided enough heat for all of the contents to burn.

"Looks like doctorates burn well," Simon said with a slight smile. He walked from the room and made his way upstairs to his own room to gather his own diplomas. On the way back, he entered Harris's room to collect his. Upon returning to the kitchen, he handed Harris the certificates which belonged to him and threw his own into the sink, frame and all. "Might as well add mine to the fire."

Frederick and Simon looked to Harris as they noted his hesitation.

"There are no doctors here, Harris," Frederick said solemnly. "It's just us, just the men beneath the man-made layers."

Harris wordlessly threw his documents into the fire, smiling as he nodded to the other two.

"I kind of wish the student loan people could see us now," Harris said with a smirk. They all enjoyed a brief chuckle.

"There's one more thing we have to cast off," Frederick said.

"The house," Simon replied. Frederick nodded.

"Do we set it on fire?" Harris asked.

"I don't think we need to destroy it. I think we need to just leave it behind," Frederick replied. He walked to the kitchen door, situated on the south side of the house. He opened it to expose the cloud of white light that broke through the dark abyss. Harris and Simon walked over to look around him.

"It looks miles away," Simon said.

"Only if you hold onto our mortal notions of time and space," Frederick said.

"So we should jump?" Harris asked.

"No, we should just walk out there," Frederick replied.

"What if we fall?" Harris asked.

"What if we don't?" Simon interrupted.

"Let's do it together," Harris said.

"We can't. We have to leave behind what we valued in the world," Frederick said.

"So we have to go individually?" Simon asked.

"That's how we came into the world," Frederick said. "If the three of us try to do it together, we might inadvertently drag along someone who isn't ready. We can't force anyone to walk. We have to go it alone."

"Do you think we'll see each other on the other side?" Simon asked.

"Probably not. We don't need bodies or images over there. We don't need to discuss politics any longer. Over there is an amazing light. We broke off from that light like little sparks when we were born. Now, we're rejoining the power source." Frederick said.

"I'm going to miss you guys," Simon said sadly.

"Frederick's right. Our energy wasn't destroyed with our body, but it is going to transfer back to the source of all energy. We may not see each other. We may not see our families. But we are joining with them and with everyone who ever walked the earth. It isn't going to be like the movies where we all hug and reunite, but that's kind of the point. We need to get rid of that notion. What we are about to do is going to be different from anything we could ever imagine."

"I know, I'm trying to get my mind around that," Simon replied.

"You should stop trying. Logic won't help us understand this problem. We can't analyze what we are about to do. What lies ahead is not observable by the physical senses. We left behind the days of cost-benefit analyses in the mortal world. Maybe we just become pure energy. Maybe Harris's right and we'll just wake up in a hospital. Maybe we reincarnate. Or maybe there are harps after all. But to get over there, we have to leave here," Frederick said. He then turned around and placed a hand on each of his friends' shoulders. "Goodbye, guys, " He said as he withdrew his hands. He backed up on the porch before turning around to face the white light and continued walking forward. He disappeared from the view of the others. No dramatic fall was to be seen. Neither did the light engulf him. His disappearance would leave more questions than answers as to what lay beyond those steps. Simon nodded as he looked into the void that had once contained his friend and smiled. He patted Harris on the arm and looked at him.

"Catch you later, man. Have fun being pure energy or whatever," Simon said with a smile as he walked down the porch steps. He simply disappeared once he reached the bottom. Harris turned around to look at the house. He remembered the days of his life where he had leaned against that granite countertop as he debated politics with his friends. He recalled days of smoking cigars in the living room while discussing mutual funds. But he realized that those days had passed. He could never go back. There was nowhere to go but forward, no matter what the future would bring. With a smile he confidently strode across the porch and ran down the painted wooden stairs. He found himself laughing as he stepped into the void.

Red Scare

The sound of Buddy Holly filled the dark basement as Eric sat at his makeshift workbench. The humming glow of his desk lamp provided the only source of light in the house and was directed at the scattered bits of electronic components and cheap tools. Lingering cigarette smoke refracted the light to obscure Eric's view even more than the dirty coke bottle lenses on his sweaty face. A cigarette dangled from his lips, quivering slightly as he attempted to concentrate through frustration on his task. Eric's goal was simple; he wanted to block the radio signals that were being transmitted into his mind by aliens. His efforts were hindered by an extremely limited knowledge of electronics and the fact that the aliens who oppressed him were simply figments of his demented mind. After a few more minutes of attempting to force his newly made device into the back of a radio, Eric threw his screwdriver across the room in frustration and stood up. He puffed heavily on his cigarette before extinguishing it on the edge of the wooden table.

"I'm hungry," said the voice.

"Leave me alone," Eric replied.

"Come on, how about a burger?"

"If you want a burger, come down and get one."

"Nah, you eat it. Then we can both enjoy it."

Eric knew that arguing with his mental captor was useless. These sorts of discussions could last for hours and his nameless nemesis seemed to have much more patience than he did. Besides, he was kind of hungry also. Eric walked up the stairs to the main floor of his slice of working class paradise. His father gave the railroads the better part of his time on Earth to bequeath it to his only son. Eric pulled a khaki colored Eisenhower style jacket over his sweaty white undershirt and walked out. IT was for the best, anyway, his house depressed him. It had remained virtually unchanged since the death of his mother a year prior. It was a dusty shrine to a dead family where Eric still felt he couldn't eat in the living room without permission. He made his way out to the driveway and approached the driver's side door of the 1950 Henry J that sat in the gravel driveway amidst untrimmed weeds and neighborhood debris. Eric climbed in and started the car, feeling about as uncomfortable as he did in the house. He still thought of it as his father's car. It was the elder Eric's gift to himself on the occasion of his retirement. He bought it brand new and it was to last him the rest of his life. He was right. He took delivery of the car in August, was diagnosed with inoperable cancer in September and was dead just a week shy of Halloween. Every day since that Eric Jr. drove the car and subconsciously viewed it as a moving memorial to his dead father and his unfulfilled American dream. Now, nearly 8 years later, his mother was also gone and he had to drive the thing all by himself.

"Hurry up, I'm hungry," the alien said.

"I'm going as fast as I can."

"No you're not. Speed it up before I get cranky."

Eric grumbled to himself as he drove the ten minutes to Sparky's drive-in. Here, Eric was gripped with a dilemma. He could eat inside and be around people, his least favorite species of life, or eat in his father's mobile coffin. As he pulled into Sparky's, the choice became easier for him. No sooner did he arrive than the eyes of the local youths were drawn to Eric. It wasn't difficult to imagine why. Originally an elegent black, Eric painted his father's Henry J with a light beige house paint. He did it the day after his mother was buried because he felt that the lead paint might help keep the alien transmissions out of the car. It didn't work.

"They're laughing at you, Eric."

"I know."

"They're just like the kids in school, aren't they?"

Eric felt his pulse quickening as his heart fluttered. The same arrhythmia that prevented his service during both the second World War and Korea now caused his skin to crawl with the tingly sting of embarrassment at the thought of remaining within sight of the abusive glares and crippling laughter. He parked and went inside.

The music was loud and the place was packed. Laughter and cigarette smoke filled the air and Eric was fortunate enough to find refuge in a booth in the corner. The music and the laughter put him even more on edge. However, he knew that his alien overlord was less likely to transmit to him in front of this many people.

"What can I getcha?" the waitress asked.

"Uhh..a cheeseburger and a malt, please."

The waitress scrawled down the order and walked off without another word. Eric was glad. The last thing he needed right now was banter. Eric took his alone time to focus on his twiddling thumbs. He had considered that there were no aliens at all. Perhaps the transmissions into his mind were the doings of the Soviets. He dismissed that idea because the voice had no accent; Eric prided himself on detecting accents however slight they might be. Still, he couldn't live with these transmissions forever. No matter the source of the alien voices, he couldn't run the risk of any foreign force spying on him at work and at home. Who knows how many secrets he had already involuntarily passed along to the aliens? His thoughts were interrupted by the receipt of his burger and drink. He ate them hungrily, drawing the disgusted looks of the local youth once again as he chewed quickly and without the benefit to others of closing his mouth during the process. He left his money on the table and made a swift exit to his car as if he had stolen something and needed to escape.

As he drove down the road he turned on the radio sending the sounds of Benny Goodman through the car. But after a minute, he flipped the radio off and was dismayed to hear that, once again, it continued playing after turning it off. This was a game the aliens played with him sometimes.

"I thought you liked Benny Goodman?"

"I don't want to listen to music right now," Eric said. His voice was slightly irritated as he spoke.

"Thanks for the burger. It was pretty good wasn't it?"

"It was fine."

"Oh come on, don't be sore. You needed to eat lunch anyway."

"I just want you to leave me alone."

"Come on, pal. You don't want me to go away. What if I told you a secret?"

The Henry J pulled into the dilapidated driveway and the engine shut down. Eric sat still for a moment as he contemplated the offer.

"What sort of secret?"

"I know you're thinking of telling someone about me."

Chills ran down Eric's spine as he heard this. It was true. Lingering fears that this was all a soviet spy game had convinced Eric that he wanted no part of it. He didn't want to be accused of treason or aiding the enemy. What he wanted was to be left alone.

"I don't know what you're talking about."

"Sure you do. In fact, I know you were debating whether you should tell the police or go straight to the Air Force. "

"Well why shouldn't I?" Eric asked in an elevated tone.

"And tell 'em what, Pal? That the aliens are sending signals into your brain that only you can hear? They'll lock you up for good and you know it. They put your aunt away for telling tales that sounded half as crazy as that."

Eric kicked open the door of the car and stormed inside. He removed his coat quickly and tossed it onto the couch as he made his way toward the basement.

"The sofa is not a closet!" his mother's voice called out. Eric's footsteps stopped suddenly. He repentantly returned to the sofa and picked up his jacket which he hung up in the hall closet.

"Sorry mother," he said contritely. He continued into the basement where the radio continued to play. He returned to the workbench where his project radio and the assorted electronic parts remained scattered. He pushed aside the various pieces of his insane puzzle and placed a piece of paper on the table. He turned up his radio to block out the alien signals as he began writing. This was to be the letter to end the Cold War. Aliens or Soviets, it didn't really matter. One way or the other, the transmissions were going to stop.

The letter was handwritten over the constant objections of the aliens. Eric had to turn up the radio twice to help drown out their ranting. That didn't exactly help his concentration but he was able to compose what, he felt, was a well thought out and logical report of the alien communications and how they likely tied back to a secret Soviet spy program. Sealed into an envelope and addressed to the Pentagon, Eric was one step closer to freedom.

"They'll think you're crazy."

"Or they'll hail me as a hero for catching some reds trying to steal our thoughts."

"Oh come on, Eric. I'm no communist. I'm a republican."

"They got republicans wherever you're from?"

"Why is that so hard to believe?"

Eric ignored the question as he marched the envelope to the mailbox on the corner. Depositing it inside, he returned to his living room where he sunk down to the spot on the floor near the radio he had occupied since childhood.

"Wanna hear another secret, Eric?"

"Go away."

"Oh come on. I thought you liked secrets?"

"Fine. Go ahead and tell me. But I don't have to believe a damn thing you say."

"The reds are coming for you, Eric. It's gonna be bad. Worse than Pearl Harbor, even."

"You said you weren't a communist."

"I'm not, but I can see what they're doing too. They're coming for you, pal. And if you think sending letters to the government is going to help, you're in for a rude awakening."

Eric rubbed his knees nervously as he considered the thought. He walked upstairs to the master bedroom, left untouched following his mother's death, and went into the closet where he began to dig through a large trunk.

"You better not be going through my things, son," his father's voice called out.

"I'm not, Dad. I'm just looking for something."

"I hope you're being straight with me, kid. If I find out you're lying, I'll give you a fresh one. I don't care if you're over thirty!"

Eric sighed and ignored the voice as he dug through the trunk. A stack of uniforms on the left side of the trunk served as a reminder of the decades the elder Eric spent as a railroad cop. And tucked away in a cigar box at the bottom was the .38 special he carried during his last years on the job. A flip of the latch released the cylinder. Eric peeked inside to verify that it was unloaded. He sat back against the doorframe of the closet as he dug out a half full box of .38 rounds and loaded the revolver as his father had taught him when he was twelve years old. The cylinder snapped back into place with a click and like a hypnotist's snap, his anxiety disappeared suddenly. Eric exhaled with relief as he held the loaded weapon in his hand. Tucking it into his waistband, he moved back downstairs to his basement retreat.

"Are you feeling big and strong now, Eric?"

"I'm not afraid of you."

"Why? Because you have six whole bullets? Do you think that will stop the reds?"

"I'll be fine."

"So, you have one for Kruschev; one for Kim Il-Sung ; and four for all of their armies, do ya?"

"Shut up."

"Just trying to offer friendly advice."

"I don't need your help," Eric said. His anxiety was slowly starting to creep back. But it was important that he didn't let on that he was becoming distressed. The aliens might know his thoughts but, as far as he could tell, they couldn't read his feelings. He was just preparing to descend the steps to the basement when he heard a knock at the door. Eric froze and he felt that arrhythmic heart flutter once again. He walked to the door slowly, his hand wrapping around the pistol's grip. He tucked it into the back of his waistband to conceal it from the view of his visitor. He carefully peered through the window beside the door. There, two policemen stood wearing navy blue uniform. Eric breathed a sigh of relief and opened the door.

"Afternoon, are you Eric?"

"Yes, sir. How can I help you?"

"Just stopped by to say hello. One of your neighbors just wanted us to check in on you, see if you were doing OK."

"I'm fine."

"I went to the academy with an Eric Smith. Any relation?" the older officer asked.

"He was my father. He died about eight years ago."

"Sorry to hear that, son," he said.

"Can't help but notice the interesting paint job on your car. Do that yourself?" the younger officer asked.

"Yes, I did."

"Well, I hate to pry in a man's business. But can I ask why you did it? I'll bet that was a pretty handsome car with its original paint."

Eric's eyes darted back and forth and sweat began to form along his hairline. He looked to the mailbox, realizing that there was no way his letter made it to the Pentagon yet, it having been deposited within the last hour.

"Looks like our first comrade is here…" the voice said softly. Eric's eyes widened as he focused on the younger officer's nametag. In white block letters it spelled out the name "KARPINSKI." Eric reached up and wiped the sweat from his brow.

"I guess I don't know much about car painting…" Eric said weakly to the officer, trying to play it cool as the aliens transmitted to him.

"What do you do for a living, son?" the older officer asked.

"Next thing they'll want to see your papers, Eric. That's usually how the gestapo operates. The reds are here, Eric." Eric gulped heavily as he attempted to compose himself. His normal anxiety was exacerbated by the alien naggings. His heart palpitated as he looked to the officer, finding his words caught in his throat.

"You all right, son?" the officer asked. Eric suddenly found his footing once again. Reaching behind him he withdrew the revolver while simultaneously cocking the hammer with his thumb. The first round went into the younger officer's chest while the pistol was still in motion. Eric made a point of taking out Karpinski first. The older officer made a motion to draw his own firearm but Eric was faster. A single round struck the officer's right shoulder, sending him back against the porch banister. In the split second before the third shot was sent through his forehead, Eric took note of the look of shock in the officer's eyes.

"Good job, Eric. You gave those old reds hell," the alien said. Eric closed the front door and locked it. He placed the barrel of the revolver, still hot from its recent firing, against the temple of his head.

"I told you to shut up!" he yelled before a tug of his index finger brought an end to these alien intrusions once and for all.

SUBWAY

Paul sat on the plastic seats of the One Train. It arrived, for the fourth time since he boarded, at the South Ferry Station.

BING BONG

The passengers disembarked as they headed for their lives of purpose and rushed to meet their oh-so-precious deadlines. Men in suits and women in scrubs all walked past him, presumably heading to the ferry upstairs. They were all so very busy.

But Paul stayed behind. He didn't drown out the sounds of the city with his headphones or the smells of the city with cheap cologne. By his estimations, he had traveled nearly 100 miles by train along the same stretch of track. He had seen the same stations from South Ferry to Van Cortlandt Park. He watched the delays intently and he absorbed every sight and smell along the way.

Sunlight or smog, it didn't matter. Paul watched as though he were in a world apart from the lemming people on the train. Like Pavlov's dog, they responded to that familiar chime at each stop.

BING BONG

The doors would open.

BING BONG

The doors would close.

"Stand clear of the closing doors," the recorded voice would say. It was often the closest thing to a conversation he heard. Sometimes the tourists would break the silence.

"Can I transfer to the 'R' from this station?" they would ask. Paul would ignore them. If he helped, they would never learn.

"Is it this stop for the Statue of Liberty?" they would ask. Eric remained silent. They probably didn't even know it was on an island.

Sometimes when the train would stop, Eric would look across the platform to the other set of tracks.

BING BONG

Maybe he could get up and run. If he leapt onto the tracks at the right moment, it would break the monotony of the whole damn process. But he never does it.

They say that New York is the city that never sleeps. But it is never fully awake, either. New York is like that sucky state of being when you first wake up. You realize the dreams weren't real but reality still feels somewhat distant. Always teetering between consciousness and sleep, New York thrives on routine. That routine is like a carousel that Paul has grown tired of. But the reality is that he, like all of the other subway passengers, will never step off.

They'll drink their fancy coffee and make fun of places like Oklahoma for not being as enlightened or cultured as New York. They'll eat street food from countries that ceased to exist after their last civil war decades ago and wear the clothing once owned by the elderly. Old becomes vintage and strange becomes exotic.

But Paul and his friends will delight in their own enlightenment. They will bask in their self-proclaimed freedom as they walk streets under constant surveillance. They will admire the public spaces to which they feel entitled yet walk through them on egg shells fearing a fine for any of the myriad offenses which keep the public safe.

They are the elite. They are the enlightened. They can be anything they want to be or nothing at all just to be ironic. They rely on the lower rents of the outer boroughs and their parents' health insurance plan. They are both the present and the future.

BING BONG

Yet, without realizing it, they move only when prompted. Paul looked behind the curtain. He saw the show for what it really was; it wasn't magic, it was just an illusion. And that depressed the hell out of him.

The Fall of Olympus

Zeus sat high atop Olympus and sighed. His stomach growled with hunger as he gazed into the sacred pool to look upon the humans. He watched as his temples, and those of his siblings and children, were desecrated. His most devoted followers embraced the new cult with fervor. Those were refused soon found themselves an oppressed minority. His gaze was interrupted by brief series of coughs from behind him. He turned to look at the failing body of Ares seated in his throne. Once strong and fierce, he now grew weak from the lack of offerings from the humans.

Hephaestus fell first. The craftsmen were the first to embrace the new cult. He found no offerings. His wisdom was not sought. His crippled legs prevented him from retreating to Olympus to be with the rest. A single tear formed in Zeus's eye at the thought of him dying alone. It slid down the mighty cheek of the King of the Gods before being wiped away by the back of his hand. He looked upon the vacant thrones.

Hades. Oh the trouble Hades caused when he was on Olympus. The Olympians had thought that Hades, above all, would survive the great purge. After all, his damned souls would remain under his control. But the angels of the new God broke down the gates of the underworld and freed the damned. They imprisoned the heroes of the Elysian Fields. Hades was now bound with great chains and condemned to suffer in his own domain. Like Prometheus before him he could not die; he could only exist in agony.

"Father, I am going to descend to Earth. I will bring us food and warmth," Athena said softly. Zeus had refused to descend the mountain himself. He feared he would happen upon the corpse of Hera, who had thrown herself to her death to escape the hunger and indignity.

"Go, but don't worry about us, dear daughter. Now is the time to save yourself," Zeus replied. Athena simply stepped back and left the palace. Zeus sighed as he realized he would never see Athena again. He could only hope that she could dwell in peace and be spared the fate that awaited him. He returned his gaze to the pool and waved his arm over the pure waters to recast the images before him. The mariners too had lost faith. This would cause much pain to Poseidon. Hopefully, he would find greater security in his kingdom than Olympus was able to afford. But the rest had either died or deserted. Hopefully those who deserted would survive. Zeus never imagined that such a thing could happen. This was so unlike his overthrow of his own father's rule. This was a stab at the heart of the very essence of the gods. This was a massacre aimed to eliminate their divine bloodline from the Earth.

As the daylight began to fade there was a sudden flash of lightning. Zeus looked up. Olympus sat high above the clouds and the only lightning he had known came from his fist. But this did not. He stood up and walked to the threshold of his palace.

The sound of unsheathed metal could be heard. He turned in time to see Ares drive the blade of his sword into his stomach. He winced and his shoulders slumped. He turned back to the entrance. There, legions of angels approached his heavenly abode and he stood ready to surrender or simply be slaughtered. At this point, it didn't really matter. One angel set foot on the steps leading to the palace first. A flaming sword held tightly in his hand.

"Are you Zeus, God of the Greeks?"

"I am."

"I am Michael. How do you receive us?"

"I am hoping we can negotiate a peaceful surrender," Zeus said confidently. Michael smiled as he followed the King of the Gods into the palace. "I want only peace for those Gods and Goddesses who are still alive."

"They may be granted peace, but not as immortals. If any of your subjects enter the sacred waters and pledge themselves to our God, they will live the remainder of their days as mortals and be granted peace in the afterlife," Michael assured. He sheathed his sword and crossed his arms as he looked to Zeus. "Those who choose to remain immortal may do so provided they swear never to attempt to reclaim their place in the eyes of the humans. And, of course, we will make suitable arrangements to ensure they do not."

"I thank you for your mercy. I ask only that, as you encounter each of my children, you give them that choice and allow them to make a decision in good faith."

"Very well, we can do this for your children. But you will have to come with us," Michael said as he placed a palm on the hilt of his sword. Zeus looked around his throne room a final time and nodded. He walked with Michael to the steps where he was swept up by the angels.

Some of the remaining gods and goddesses sacrificed their divinity for the sake of life. Others could not relinquish their immortality and were simply stripped of all power and prestige. The word communicated to the masses was that the Olympians were dead. That was certainly true of many of them. However, no one of the mortal race knew what became of Zeus or how his captors treated him upon taking him from Olympus. The great palace atop Mt. Olympus was destroyed. Most of the humans carried on without noticing. Many of their temples remained, though now were dedicated to the God of a foreign land.

From his island prison off of the Nordic peninsula, Apollo warmed his hands by the fire. He took solace in knowing that the new believers would never fully crush the legacy of his people. His time to reign had ended; though his time to reflect had begun.

Preppers

Michael did his best to put on a brave face for the others in the shelter. He sat on a concrete bench as casually as his rigid body would permit and focused on suppressing the trembling of his hands. Every few seconds the lights would flicker. It sounded as if a whole fleet of trains were passing just overhead. If only they were trains, Michael thought. He looked to the others in the shelter. Some were praying. Others were crying. Michael could hardly blame them, though he didn't see the point in either activity. His body was nervous as it feared harm. His mind, however, was reconciled to that fact that this could be his final day.

As he looked around the subterranean shelter, he couldn't help but wonder if he had been right. He looked at every joint and hinge and wondered if his calculations and estimates had been accurate. He found himself questioning some of those more minute details and cursing himself for not having investigated further before today. It reminded him of turning in a math test as a kid. Once the paper was handed in, it was too late to second guess. The only difference here was that a failure would result in the death of all of those hiding. Oh well, there was nothing he could do about it now.

Four nearly ten years Michael had prepared for the end. He saw the warning signs of a planet in decay and a society marching loudly toward its end. Different people prepare for the end of days in their own way. Some simply choose to embrace the moment and live life fully. But Michael, and others like him, choose instead to try to live through the disaster to live their final days in a simple post-civilization way.

"I don't think it will hold!" Henry yelled across the narrow aisle separating him from Michael.

"Too late to worry about it now!" Michael yelled back. The outside noise was deafening and the rattle of the simple interior fixtures inside the cylindrical shelter rattled all the louder.

"How long does a tornado last?" Henry yelled back.

"Sometimes a few minutes. Other times, over an hour. Hard to tell. The weather is doing all sorts of screwed up stuff these days," Michael replied. Henry tried to read Michael's lips as the rattling and crashing drowned out the bulk of the reply. Henry nodded and sat back on his own concrete bench. Michael closed his eyes and found himself smiling. There was a good possibility that they would all die. But if there was a chance of survival, then those in the shelter had the best chance of walking away from the torrent of storms. It had been nearly two days and there seemed to be a tornado just overhead every few hours. Those in the shelter were worried, but those who took refuge in nearby basements were likely all dead. Michael wasn't smiling because of their demise, per se. But those were the people who told him he was crazy and that the surge of storms would never come. He knew he was right and these past two days validated his abilities as a survivor and lent credibility to his claims as a leader. The storms would pass leaving behind a trail of destruction in the process. For now, all they could do was wait.

The sound outside slowly came to a conclusion as it had done with dozens of twisters in the previous two days. The outside fell into an eerie calm. Michael picked up his stopwatch and set the timer. A clipboard beside him contained the time elapsed between tornadoes over the past few days. The most time elapsed was three hours and the least amount of time was twenty minutes.

"Should we take a look?" Henry asked.

"Too dangerous. For all we know, the second you open that hatch, the cell will just be touching down right over us," Michael replied.

"When can we look outside?"

"Let's give it an hour. One quick look and we'll play it from there."

Henry nodded. Michael leaned back and closed his eyes again. The only sound he could hear was the slowly subsiding sobs of some of his other bunker mates. After only twenty minutes, Michael's eyes opened as his ears detected a subtle but enchanting sound.

"Birds," Michael murmered.

"What?" Henry asked.

"I hear birds," Michael responded. He stood up and climbed the metal ladder to the bunker's only hatch. Two small pipes provided air, but only one hatch allowed access to the bunker. As he neared the hatch, the sound of birds became louder. Michael smiled as he wrapped his hand around the locking level and pulled it to an open position. He pushed up on the hatch only to find that it could only open about three inches. No matter, it was enough to see outside. The sun was shining and birds could be seen perching on a series of fallen trees.

"How does it look up there?" Henry asked.

"Beautiful. A regular Garden of Eden," Michael said.

"Good, let's get out there and get some fresh air and replenish the water," Henry said.

"Hold on, the hatch is caught on something," Michael said as he lowered and raised the hatch trying to push free the obstruction. Unseen by Michael, however, was the fallen oak situated just above the hatch. It had been not so delicately placed by the forces of nature just across the shelter's only means of egress. It would be no great obstacle for a small rescue squad or even a band of helpful neighbors with a chainsaw. However, Michael kept the location of his bunker secret to prevent looters from finding him in times of chaos. The passage leading up to the flip up hatch could accommodate only one person at a time, a security measure Michael instituted to prevent an invasion of his bunker by desperate marauders. The key issue with that approach being that it would take more force than all of the bunker inhabitants had at their disposal to move the tree to freedom. But for their final days, the survivors would be able to gaze upon the perfect weather that followed the storms and breathe the fresh air that made it through that three inch gap. They had made it through the tribulations to see the paradise which lay just beyond their reach.

Ruin

Originally published in the *Under the Knife* anthology by Cruentus Libri Press.

Angela couldn't help but observe the sights and sounds of the hospital as she walked down the hallway. She had been employed as in-house counsel for the Atlantic Metropolitan Hospital for four years. She was grateful to have found such a stable job. She knew how difficult it could be to land a position like this, especially considering she had only served as an associate for four years following law school.

She loved the fact that her office wasn't a glass tower filled with lawyers clawing their way to the top. Instead, she was one of three attorneys in a world of doctors, nurses and a seemingly endless support staff. There, she enjoyed the prestige of being one of the few legal experts on site. She was a big legal fish in a small pond. Secretly, she also felt quite the thrill at how her appearance could disarm even the cockiest of surgeons and the most arrogant of administrators. No one ever wanted to see legal coming toward them. Her shoes clicked against the vinyl composite tile floor, pristinely waxed to a high gloss. She smiled and nodded in greeting as she passed nurses stations and patient rooms. She loved it when the nurses would pause to watch her. She could sense their pulses quickening as they waited to see if they were the purpose of Angela's visit. But Angela wasn't there to see nurses about a complaint. She wasn't there to address an accusation of stolen jewelry or to get a patient to sign a waiver that was missed during admission.

She was there to end a career.

Angela's own heart beat rapidly in anticipation as she practiced her best lawyer speech in her own mind. She had never met Dr. Smith in person before. His name was known to her only through a paper file she had been slowly compiling over the past two years. Dr. Smith was well regarded as a physician during the course of his twenty three years of practice at Atlantic Metropolitan. He graduated at the top of his class from an Ivy League medical school. He served as a deacon in his church. He had a wife and some kids and had coached little league and gone on scouting trips. He was the perfect model of a doctor and citizen. And Angela was going to ruin him.

The reason for his discharge was valid according to the letter of hospital policy. Dr. Smith had taken a package of gauze from a supply closet to stock his personal medical bag before heading out to work at a free clinic. When the matter was brought to the attention of the administration, he was charged seven dollars and the matter was considered closed. Per hospital policy, a copy of the event was forwarded to legal for filing. Angela could hardly contain her delight.

For two years she had been building a case. As she approached the conference room, she tried to remember how she had fixated on the model physician. It was, perhaps, a combination of things. Dr. Smith's name first appeared on her desk as a party to a malpractice suit. A patient had died on the operating table as a result of a hemorrhage. Given the nature of his work as an anesthesiologist, Dr. Smith could not really be blamed for the death, but had been named in the suit along with the rest of the surgical team. Something drew her attention to the name on the papers. It was her perfection that sparked her suspicion. It was her suspicion which led her to near obsession. She scoured records and collected bits and pieces. She knew that no one could be so pristine. She knew there was dirt and she couldn't seem to give up the search for it.

Then Dr. Smith stole some gauze. She knew it was likely an innocent omission. It was the sort of temporary lapse in judgment that anyone could have made. Human resources was willing to let it go with a simple restitution, leaving him to otherwise continue his perfect career. But Angela didn't like the idea of him walking away.

"Had this same incident involved a first year nurse, she would have been terminated on the spot."

Angela had argued to the Vice President of Human Resources.

Yet they still refused to take action. No matter. Angela had taken the initiative to resolve the matter herself. The thirty year old wrapped her hand around the brushed nickel handle leading into the fourth floor conference room and smiled as she stepped off of the tile and onto the maroon carpet. A rush of cold air from the over-zealous air conditioner hit her with a frigid blast as her eyes fell upon the man seated at the table. He was in his fifties and was exactly the man Angela had pictured. He was tall and handsome and his body was fit. His attire was professional but not flashy. He was as perfect as his file indicated. Angela smiled.

The man rose and extended a hand to her. Angela shook his hand firmly and spoke first.

"Dr. Smith, I presume?" she said somewhat playfully.

"I'm Angela, we spoke on the phone. Please, have a seat," Angela said before he could reciprocate the greeting.

"So what is it I can do for you, Angela?" Dr. Smith asked as he leaned back in his seat, palms placed over the arm rests of the cushioned chair.

"There is a matter of some gauze," Angela said in a serious tone.

Dr. Smith laughed as he ran his hands over his brown, well groomed hair.

"Aren't we done with that? I paid the $7. I just wasn't thinking. I wanted to make sure I was stocked for doing some volunteer work."

Angela opened the folder on the table began writing notes on the first page.

"I'm afraid not. You see, even though you made restitution, surely you can understand how some people might take issue with a physician being given a free pass on taking hospital supplies when we routinely terminate clerks, nurses and janitors for the same."

"So I'm being terminated? After twenty three years a roll of gauze ends it all?" Dr. Smith asked flatly. His smile faded and his irritation was evident.

"No, you're not being terminated. I'm asking you to resign," Angela slid three pages across the glossy finish of the conference table to Dr. Smith.

"Effective thirty days from now you would resign. Because you have over twenty years of service, we can call it a retirement. We throw you a party and you walk away."

"Walk away to what?"

"That's up to you. You can start your own practice if you want. I'm sure with as distinguished a career as yours you would have no problem finding other employment, if you wish."

"And if I don't retire?" Dr. Smith crossed his arms defiantly as he looked to her.

"Then we terminate you for cause. We would also be required to inform the state disciplinary board of our actions."

Dr. Smith kept his arms crossed and bit his lower lip as he looked down to the papers thoughtfully. Angela suppressed a smile as she watched him. She knew there was risk. What she was doing didn't have the blessing of Human Resources. If Dr. Smith did anything other than sign the papers and fade into the sunset, she ran a very real possibility of losing her own job.

She felt immediate relief as Dr. Smith pulled a pen from his shirt pocket. He clicked the point forward with a move of his thumb and signed the three pages, sliding them over to her.

"Thank you, Doctor. I'm sorry it had to come to this." Angela said with mock sincerity.

"I'm sure you're devastated. I've been considering teaching, maybe this is just God opening a window while you close the door."

This caused Angela to smile. She settled into her atheism in her third year of undergraduate studies. It never ceased to both amaze and amuse her at how religious people readily spun their tragedy into false hope.

"Perhaps." she replied with a smile.

Dr. Smith was the first to stand and Angela followed suit. They shook hands a final time.

"I'm sorry we couldn't meet under better circumstances, Doctor."

Dr. Smith shrugged as he released her hand.

"These things happen," he said with a slight smile before departing.

Angela sat in the conference room and basked in her accomplishments. She felt mildly guilty for ruining a man who hadn't really done anything wrong. Then again, she didn't really ruin him. Though his career at the hospital had ended, he would undoubtedly land on his feet. Men like Dr. Smith always landed on their feet. Angela stood up and gathered the forms, walking triumphantly through the hall as she headed back to the administration wing. It was Friday afternoon and she pondered the notion of going home early in celebration. As she arrived at her office, a modest and windowless space she sat in her chair and tucked the folder into her desk drawer. She inhaled deeply as her heart began to return to a normal pace and smiled. She had single handedly taken down a respected physician for no reason other than the fact that she wanted to.

"I'm like a freakin' legal super hero," she said aloud.

The next morning, Angela awoke in her bed still feeling the power coursing through her veins. She felt like an empress and that was a feeling she didn't want to give up. It was Saturday morning and it was beautiful outside. Her small house was only half decorated as it was a constant work in progress. Angela slipped out of bed and walked into the kitchen. She set the coffee pot brewing for a single cup of a bold roast and walked to the entryway to the unfinished den.

The room was in horrible disrepair, but Angela could only see its potential. She wanted to fill it with dark woods and leather chairs, giving it the feel of a Supreme Court Justice's chambers. She smiled as she considered the finished product.

She inhaled deeply as the aroma of her brewing coffee filled the space.

"Maybe a jog after coffee," she mused aloud.

Walking to the coffee pot she poured a fresh cup took a sip. She returned to the den and resumed her fantasy. Angela sighed as she looked to the wood paneling she had applied to the far wall. The upper right hand corner was peeling back from the wall slightly. Walking over she gave it a push with her free hand to verify that it was an easy fix. Then she picked up a cordless nail gun from the white two-step ladder beside her and took two steps up. Holding the coffee in her left hand and the nail gun in her right, she nailed the errant corner down and took a celebratory sip of coffee as she admired her work.

One step back was taken to descend the step ladder and return to the safety of the flat and level ground. But a misplaced foot caused her to trip. Though the fall was only around six inches as her feet clamored to keep her upright, it caused her to jerk her upper body and nearly drop the nail gun. She was able to awkwardly catch it with her right hand. In doing so, however, she accidentally discharged a single nail into the left side of her chest.

Angela cried out as the nail made quick work of tearing into the fibrous web of her pectoralis major and caused her to drop the coffee cup to the floor. Insult was added to injury as the cup shattered, splattering hot coffee all over her leg. She fell against the wall as she looked down to examine the damage that was done. The nail so neatly pinned her pajamas to her chest. She was afraid to move. While she certainly was a physician, the thought of the nail moving around in there seemed like it could worsen the condition. With tear stained eyes she made her way to the kitchen and picked up her cell phone from the table.

The blood spot around the nail was growing, but Angela took solace in the fact that she was under the care of people who knew best how to handle the emergency as she sat in the back of the ambulance. With any luck, this was something that could be tended to in an hour and the worst of it was behind her, leaving the remainder of the weekend to recuperate.

As she watched the street through the back windows of the ambulance, she even considered taking Monday and Tuesday off just to compensate for the lost weekend. Angela had not been to the emergency room since she was in high school and managed to fall face first while running track. It was not a place she intended to visit again. Fortunately for her, the ER seemed to consider a nail in the chest a serious enough injury to treat in an expedient manner. There were X-rays and there were vitals being taken. And then, just as quickly as she arrived, the gurney began to move down the hallway.

"Angela? I'm Dr. Walters. How are you feeling?" a middle aged woman said as she walked alongside the gurney.

"Been better, what's going on?"

"The nail came very close to your heart. We think it missed it entirely, but we need to get you into surgery to make sure it didn't cause any damage."

"Am I getting out of here today?"

"Not today. But if it missed your heart, you should be out by Monday."

Angela groaned. So much for her weekend. It struck her as a bit odd that the loss of her weekend seemed to be more troubling to her than the impending surgery. Then again, it was just a nail. Only slightly worse than stapling your finger, she reasoned. Besides, surgery has come a very long way over the last century or so.

"This will make you feel a little loopy," a nurse said as she injected something into the IV.

Sure enough, after about a minute, she began to feel warm and fuzzy and a smile returned to her face. The gurney came to a stop and a man in scrubs placed a mask over her nose and mouth.

"Just breathe normally, Angela. You're going to be just fine," the voice said.

Angela squinted her eyes, trying to focus. The voice sounded familiar, but she couldn't quite place it.

"By the way, I stopped over in Human Resources after our meeting," the doctor said simply.

Angela's eyes widened slightly.

"Shit, I'm going to get fired," was the thought that ran through her mind just before fading into sleep.

Angela awoke slowly from the haze of anesthesia. Her eyes opened partially as she looked down to her form on a hospital bed with a blanket pulled over her. She was partially propped up. Her mind still felt groggy and her body felt like it was made of lead.

"See? No big deal on the surgery," she thought to herself. All of the sudden the anxiety returned to her at the thought of losing her job over the Dr. Smith matter. It was Saturday, she would have to wait until Monday. Maybe since she was a hospital employee they would bring her up to her office. If there was trouble, she probably had some indication of it already. A voicemail, an e-mail, something had to be floating out there. Angela went to look about the room to look for a nurse or someone she could plead her case to. She was troubled by the fact that her head didn't turn. She made an effort to move her right hand. Her heart sank again as she stared at the hand as it rested lifelessly beside her.

"NURSE!" she screamed.

Yet, she heard nothing. Not the sound of her own voice or the echo of a scream.

"HELP!" she screamed again.

Despite screaming with all of her might, she could not muster even the slightest vibration of her vocal chords. Angela fell into a full panic as her continued experiments yielded no results. She was cut off from her limbs and voice. She couldn't turn her head. She was trapped.

After what seemed to be an eternity of inward panic, Dr. Smith entered the room. He pulled a chair over to her bedside, ensuring it was positioned within her limited field of vision. Unlike their meeting the day prior, he wore scrubs. He was relaxed and smiled reassuringly.

Maybe it's just a side effect of the anesthesia. Angela thought hopefully to herself.

"Good, you're awake," he said, noting that her eyes were slightly open.

"It may not seem so, but this actually worked out for the best." Dr. Smith said as he propped his feet up on the edge of the bed and leaned back as he looked to her.

"First, I have no intentions of retiring. I stopped by human resources and made a few casual inquiries into the gauze incident. Everyone there assured me the matter was closed. So I'm not sure whose behalf you were acting upon. And second, your swagger was starting to bother me. You walked the halls like a prison guard lording over his charges. You sat high atop your legal tower. Doctors fear you. Oh yes they do. When you walk down the hall, everyone's heart skips a beat. Not anymore. I suppose I should have just reported you.

You likely would have been fired. Maybe you would have been disbarred. But this seems more fitting. Young, attractive and successful, I can't explain it, really. I wanted to crush you just because you were there."

Angela's blood ran cold as she stared blankly at Dr. Smith. It was becoming apparent that her present condition was likely not temporary.

"It's surprisingly easy to redirect EEG results, especially when you've been around this place as long as I have. They'll figure out that you're somewhere inside there, eventually. I have no doubt of that. Of course, it may be months or years before they notice a blink. But if you can get the attention of a particularly attentive nurse or an idealistic intern, you may get them to order another test."

Dr. Smith began picking a hang nail on his left thumb, focusing his eyes on that task as he continued to speak.

"Then one day maybe you can get one of those computers so you can form words with your eyes and communicate with the outside world. That could be your second opportunity to get rid of me, I suppose. That should give you something to work for."

Dr. Smith smiled as he kicked his feet off of the edge of her bed and stood. His smile was sinister and caused Angela to feel the full impact of her condition. She watched as he walked from her limited field of vision.

Angela wanted to scream and cry. She wanted to leap up and tear Dr. Smith apart. But all of the rage and anguish did not come out in screams and thrashing. There was only silence. She found herself unable to muster so much as a mournful groan or a grunt of frustration. As the rage and anguish subsided, she felt like she was on the verge of weeping and yet, her eyes did not water and her throat would not release the sobs. Her mind and emotions were locked away. The world where she knew success was all around her, but an invisible divide kept them apart. Her final triumph would cause her unspoken pain all the days of her life: she had set out to ruin a life and had accomplished that goal with a lasting impact beyond all expectations.

The Jurist

Originally published in the *War is Hell* anthology by Cruentus Libri Press

Alan was admiring the near perfect humidity within the humidor on his office desk as his phone rang. He impatiently lifted the handset and placed it to his ear, composing himself long enough to formulate a calm salutation.

"Lieutenant Commander Matthews speaking. Please be advised this is a non-secure line."

His lips curled into a smile as he listened to the voice on the other end.

"Lance Corporal Evans was successfully executed a few minutes ago, sir." the speaker said.

"Very well." he said before hanging up the phone.

Alan Matthews insisted upon hearing when every death sentence ordered in one of his cases was carried out. Up until six months ago, he ensured his schedule permitted him to be present at each one. But since receiving his promotion to Lieutenant Commander and taking on the role of chief prosecutor, he had been unable to break free of his office in the Norfolk Naval Yard.

As a naval prosecutor, Alan prided himself on having the largest number of capital convictions. The fact that the nation was at war bolstered his success rates. Crimes that were punished lightly in times of peace became capital offenses.

Alan had successfully tried Lance Corporal Evans on the charge of cowardice. The young man froze as his unit went into battle on the outskirts of Baghdad. Many of his fellow marines perished that day and Alan saw to it that Evans joined the ranks of the non-living. Unlike his comrades, however, Lance Corporal Evans died without the honor associated with death in combat. Those fallen marines went home in flag draped caskets to funeral processions with local dignitaries from their hometowns in tow. Evans would be shipped to the funeral home of his family's choosing in a wooden crate. He would wear his uniform with rank insignias and unit patches torn off, like all of the other convicts Alan had seen to their graves. To Alan, this was the rightful fate of traitors.

Alan looked around his office a t the certificates and awards from a lifetime ago. He had started his career in law as an idealistic public interest attorney. Back then, he would have been far more likely to defend Corporal Evans rather than prosecute him. But when Iran invaded Iraq on May 14, 2015, the United States mobilized its forces.

When Iran took Baghdad on the first of April and aimed their nuclear warheads at Israel, the United States took to the battlefield. The draft had begun once Russia entered the war on the side of Iran and attorney Alan Matthews found himself wearing a uniform and assigned as an assistant prosecutor.

At first he resisted the iron fist nature of military justice in favor of the idealistic humanism that had guided him all of his life up to that point. But having not known material success in the area of public interest law, Alan found himself for the first time able to buy things he had always done without. He fell in love with the officer's club lifestyle and was willing to do what it took to ensure his future comfort. Promotions and medals were dangled before him like a carrot on a stick and Alan ran with all of his might to accumulate as many convictions as possible.

The first hanging he witnessed, that of a young seaman convicted of desertion, simultaneously repulsed and aroused him. Alan was mortified by the death of the human body and aroused by the fact that it was he who brought about that death.

With each conviction, Alan won notoriety and respect among his fellow lawyers and fear among the accused. It was a well known fact that, if the law contained any provision for a penalty of death in your case, Lieutenant Commander Matthews was likely to pursue it.

Alan stood from his leather chair and looked through his office window over the naval yard. Like every day that month, the sky was grey and the air was wet. Ships could be seen patrolling the harbor. Six months earlier, a Russian attack sub had been discovered nearby. Since then, the frontline had moved from the middle of the Atlantic to just off the eastern shore of the United States. That sudden shift caused quite a stir among the enlisted. Sailors and marines stateside support billets now feared coming to work. Some went on unauthorized absence and others tried to flee to Canada, a capital offense in time of war.

Alan had no sympathy for the cowards who shirked their duty. He had a duty as well, and he embraced it.

In a closed door trial on the far side of the base, Alan Matthews stood before a jury box filled with naval officers as he delivered his closing argument.

"Ensign Oliver admits that he attempted to desert the United States Navy in crossing the border into Canada. He admits that he went with no intention of returning. He admits that he went seeking political asylum from the Canadian government. He holds no remorse for having done these things. He maintains that, had he not been stopped at the border and detained, he would have gladly carried on with his plans. Sirs, Ensign Oliver's actions were selfish. They were the acts of a coward and a traitor to our nation. When his nation needed him the most, he attempted to turn his back on it. Worse yet, his being an officer is a devastating blow to morale for our enlisted. We must set an example. We must send a message to our forces that these cowardly acts will not go unpunished. We must send the message that acts of treason will be met with the most severe punishment. Military service is about duty and courage. It is about honor and dignity. Ensign

Oliver has disgraced these very principles. Our complacency with his actions will only encourage more disharmony within the ranks."

Alan walked past the defendant's table, looking upon the twenty-two year old officer in his neatly pressed uniform as he proceeded to his own seat. The defense attorney, a civilian, made no pleas of innocence on his client's behalf. He only begged for mercy.

"Elwood Oliver is twenty-two years old. Less than one year ago, he was an art history major living the college life in Colorado. He was drafted, commissioned and assigned to a command he was ill-prepared for. He does not have the temperament of a leader. He is not a coward. He, like many other individuals is simply not built for the military life. He is not built to be a naval officer. His actions undoubtedly deserve punishment. His actions have brought disgrace upon his uniform. But Elwood Oliver does not deserve to die. He does not deserve to be imprisoned for a prolonged period of time.

Remember decisions you made at his age and imagine that that you were never given a second chance. Elwood Oliver needs mercy and I pray that you all see that and will do what is right. Commander Matthews speaks of the dignity of the service. I ask that you consider the dignity of a man."

The verdict came back in less than a half hour and with it, a sentence of death by hanging. Alan Matthews caressed his leather briefcase as he smiled. The conviction of an officer would bring him added prestige. In fact, he fully intended to put himself in for a commendation upon returning to his office.

Ensign Oliver crumpled to the floor as he wept. The sound of his mother wailing from the gallery brought blows from the judge's gavel. It didn't matter. The courts-martial always ended the same. There was weeping and the occasional outburst of anger and then there was silence. The appeals process had been suspended once the war escalated and Alan could count on a swift execution of the errant young officer.

If it was Alan's intention to deny dignity to those who compromised the dignity of the navy, then death by hanging surely satiated him. Since the discovery of the Russian submarine in U.S. waters, the base held public executions to serve as an example of how not to serve one's country. Alan could not justify his presence at the hanging of Ensign Oliver. He had just received another case. A female hospital corpsman attempted to evade duty by injuring herself with a scalpel. Alan intended to pursue the most severe punishment for a malingerer in a time of war. But as he stood in his office peering through the window, just days after the conviction of Ensign Oliver, he found himself staring at the gallows erected near the pier. Sailors and marines manned the rails of their ships and stood in formation on the ground as the tiny figure approached his noose. Alan's view was obscured by distance and passing foot traffic but he knew that it was Ensign Oliver climbing the steps toward the noose. He knew as the figure dipped suddenly that the trap door had been tripped and the life of Ensign Oliver had ended. Though he was not present to witness the horrific death, he knew every detail. Like all of the others before, Ensign Oliver was wearing a uniform devoid of rank or insignias of any sort. He knew that the body convulsed as his neck snapped with the sudden jerk of the fall. He was aware that, at that moment, urine dripped from the downward turned toes of a twenty-two year old ensign and the smell of feces gagged his executioner and the attending physician nearby. The only thing he didn't know was whether Ensign Oliver cried.

It seemed a peculiar question to enter his mind. Yet, so many had ended their days at those same gallows and Alan had seen it all. Some died with quiet dignity while others went kicking and screaming. As his phone began to ring, he picked up the handset and placed it to his ear.

"Lieutenant Commander Matthews. Please be advised this is a non-secure line." he greeted flatly.

"Sir, Ensign Oliver was successfully executed." the voice offered without prompting.

"Very well." Alan was prepared to hang up as usual, but paused before speaking again. "Did he go quietly?"

"No, sir. He sang 'Anchors Aweigh.'"

"Thank you, Petty Officer."

Alan hung up the phone and looked through the window. He was perturbed by the fact that Ensign Oliver chose to sully the song of his beloved service. It was a weak attempt to steal dignity from the uniform that had been taken away just prior to his hanging. In any case, Ensign Oliver was dead and would be shipped home in the same wooden crate, devoid of any honors.

That night, Alan Matthews sat in his office smoking a celebratory cigar from the impressive humidor on the corner of his dominating desk. He was flipping through the case file of the corpsman he would soon see to the gallows. He would have to clear his schedule for her execution, he reasoned. It would be cause to celebrate. Until this point, Alan never had the opportunity to execute a woman.

"Stand Navy out to sea, fight our battle cry…" the words were sung in a low monotone.

Alan jumped in his seat, his hand moving to his chest as he felt his heart skip a beat. He looked around the office to find the originator of the shocking lyrics. He lifted the phone to his ear only to find a vacant dial tone. He looked at his watch. It was nearly 11:30 p.m., and he reasoned that any mysterious songs were a result of his own lack of sleep.

He left the papers in disarray on his desk as he walked downstairs. His stroll to the officer's barracks was uneventful. He entered his room on the south side of the base and removed his uniform cap, placing it on the counter in the kitchenette. He sighed as he began to remove his shirt.

"We'll never change our course so vicious foes steer shy-y-y…" the song continued. The voice was familiar, yet foreign to Alan's recollection. It came through as nearly whisper and seemed to come from the opposite direction in which Alan would look.

"Who the hell is there?"

"Roll out the T.N.T., anchors aweigh. Sail on to victory…"

"This is Lieutenant Commander Matthews! I don't think this is funny. Show yourself immediately!" he interrupted.

"..and sink their bones to Davy Jones hooray…"

"Goddamnit, I'm not kidding. Whoever is doing this is in big trouble. You hear me? Big trouble!"

"From the halls of Montezuma to the shores of Tripoli…" came another whispered tone.

Alan turned suddenly to try to locate the source of the singing. He would swing suddenly back as he tried frantically to find his harasser.

"Who the hell are you? What do you want?"

Both voices sang their respective fight songs simultaneously, and then others slowly joined in. Different voices began a muddled chorus of the fight songs for the Navy and Marine Corps. Unsure of what else to do, Alan placed his fingertips in his ears. Despite his fear, he found a moment of peace as his fingertips ceased the endless singing. He realized he had instinctively closed his eyes as he sought to block out the unwelcome sounds. As he opened his eyes, his heart sank as he looked upon Ensign Oliver.

The young ensign was wearing the neatly pressed uniform he had donned at his court-martial. His white uniform cap was tucked under his left arm. Despite his shock, Alan noted that he could see

Oliver mouthing the words to Anchors Aweigh. He stumbled back away from Oliver but quickly stopped when he backed into what felt like a person.

Spinning around rapidly, fingers still in his ears, he saw Lance Corporal Evans. He too was wearing the full uniform as neatly and properly as he had on the day of his condemnation. Alan fell into a chair as other sailors and marines approached. Their mouths all moved as they sang the fight song of their branch though the sound was blocked by the now shaking fingertips Alan had placed in his ears.

"What the hell do you all want?" he asked loudly, involuntarily unplugging his ears as he shook his hands to them.

"Sir, you should be aware that cursing in uniform is against the law. It brings disgrace upon the uniform." Lance Corporal Evans said, the chorus having silenced.

"You're dead. You're all dead. You can't possibly be here."

"We may have failed at serving in the military, but it seems to us you have failed at being a human being." Ensign Oliver said.

"I did my duty."

"That's what the Nazis said." a voice in the crowd of the deceased offered.

"I followed the law. I did what I needed to do in order to preserve the dignity of the service."

"But what about our dignity?" Lance Corporal Evans asked.

The chorus of fight songs again resumed and Alan quickly plugged his ears and shut his eyes.

"No! Stop it! None of you are here. This is a dream. I did nothing wrong! I did my duty! I…"

Alan found himself choking on his words. The attempt at completing his sentence caused him to gag. He opened his eyes and removed his fingers from his ears as his hands went to his own throat. He found himself unable to speak. No matter how hard he tried, his words would not come. Somehow, those men had made him mute.

That fast became a secondary concern as Alan realized he was no longer in his barracks room. It was hot and humid and the night air passed through his lungs no easier than if he had tried to breathe a bundle of wet wool. As he looked around, he realized he was standing on the corner of a city street.

Frantically, he ran up to the nearest person. A man in a business suit was standing at the corner waiting for the signal to change. Alan rushed up to him pointing at his throat and attempting to speak. The man looked shocked and horrified, he backed away as he held up his hands.

"Easy, take it easy. Whatever you want, just don't hurt me."

Alan grunted and groaned in frustration as he gestured to his throat. The man reached into his pocket and withdrew a few single dollar bills, tossing them to Alan as he stepped away backwards.

"This is all I have. I swear. Just take it. It's yours."

Alan instinctively grabbed at the dollar as it flew toward him. It was then he noticed his own hand. His arm was clad in a dusty black uniform overcoat. His hand was dirty and his nails long and with embedded deposits of filth beneath them. He quickly moved to the nearest storefront to look at his own reflection.

He was no longer clean shaven and a scraggly beard adorned his face. His hair was unkempt and his clothing was dirty and worn.

"Hey, get the hell away from my window!" an angry storekeeper yelled.

Alan moved away quickly. He wasn't sure how he had gotten wherever he was. He walked down the street frantically looking for a familiar sight. He came upon a police station and entered through the front door.

"Can I help you?" a bored police officer at the front desk asked.

Alan gestured to his throat and then made a motion indicating he needed a pen and paper. The officer seemed skeptical but slid a notepad to him with a pen. Alan nodded in thanks and began to write, turning it to face the officer.

"I am a naval officer." the pad read.

"Sure you are pal." the cop said dismissively. Alan shook his head and again put pen to paper.

"I am Lieutenant Commander Alan Matthews, United States Navy JAG Corps. I don't know how I got here, but I need to get back to base." Alan wrote.

"Look buddy, I'm not sure what you're after, but I don't really have time for this."

"Please help me! I have been serving since the war started." Alan wrote.

The officer's face seemed to soften a bit.

"Listen, pal. I appreciate your service. But you need to face the fact that the war has been over for almost three years now."

Alan looked confused. He dropped the pen on the desk and stepped away, walking back outside.

"Stand Navy out to sea…" the song began again. Alan reached up and placed his palms over his ears to block it out as he had before but to no avail. The sound of the singing was just as loud as it was without his hands over his ears.

"From the halls of Montezuma to the shores of Tripoli…" Lance Corporal Evan's voice joined in.

Soon, all of the voices began to sing as they had before. Alan held his head as tightly as he could, but nothing seemed to stop the singing. He leaned against a wall and slowly sank to the ground.

Tears formed in his eyes as he inwardly begged for an end to the voices.

Lieutenant Commander Alan Matthews, a naval prosecutor obsessed with the notion of dignity and honor was left without his as he held his head in an alleyway. With no knowledge of how he had arrived or how he would ever leave without the privilege of his voice, he found himself deprived of the very dignity he took from others.

About the Author

James Olivieri was born in Brooklyn, New York and raised in Northeastern Pennsylvania. After high school he served in the U.S. Navy for two years. Upon receiving his honorable discharge, he entered a men's Catholic religious order. After a change of heart and a reconsideration of the religion of his youth, he moved to New York and became an insurance fraud investigator. James currently lives in Upstate New York with his wife and daughter.

James's writing tends toward the dark without fitting the genre category of horror. His stories are typically morbid and rarely have a happy ending. They have been labeled as "tragedies" and "morality tales" but ultimately, they are really stories about just how badly life can suck given the right circumstances.

Originally published by Sleeping Cat Books, James almost exclusively focuses his writing efforts on short stories. He has had work published in two anthologies of Cruentus Libri Press as well as various places on the web.